MAGIC
TREE HOUSE®
#38 TIME OF THE TURTLE KING

Dear Reader,

Did you know there's a Magic Tree House® book for every kid? From those just starting to read chapter books to more experienced readers, Magic Tree House® has something for everyone, including science, sports, geography, wildlife, history . . . and always a bit of mystery and magic!

Magic Tree House®
Adventures with Jack and Annie, perfect for readers who are just starting to read chapter books.
F&P Level: M

Magic Tree House®
Merlin Missions
More challenging adventures for the experienced Magic Tree House® reader.
F&P Levels: M–N

Magic Tree House®
Super Edition
A longer and more dangerous adventure with Jack and Annie.
F&P Level: P

Magic Tree House®
Fact Trackers
Nonfiction companions to your favorite Magic Tree House® adventures.
F&P Levels: N–X

Happy reading!

Mary Pope Osborne

MAGIC TREE HOUSE®

#38 Time of the Turtle King

BY MARY POPE OSBORNE

ILLUSTRATED BY AG FORD

A STEPPING STONE BOOK™

Random House New York

Visit us on the Web!
rhcbooks.com
MagicTreeHouse.com

Educators and librarians, for a variety of teaching tools,
visit us at RHTeachersLibrarians.com

Library of Congress Cataloging-in-Publication Data
Names: Osborne, Mary Pope, author. | Ford, AG, illustrator.
Title: Time of the turtle king / by Mary Pope Osborne; illustrated by AG Ford.
Description: New York: Random House, 2023. | Series: Magic tree house; #38 |
Summary: "When the magic tree house returns it whisks Jack and Annie away to the Galapagos Islands, where they become World Turtle Experts and must save a tortoise in danger from an erupting volcano."—Provided by publisher.
Identifiers: LCCN 2022045561 (print) | LCCN 2022045562 (ebook) |
ISBN 978-0-593-48854-6 (trade) | ISBN 978-0-593-48855-3 (lib. bdg.) |
ISBN 978-0-593-48856-0 (ebook)
Subjects: CYAC: Magic—Fiction. | Tree houses—Fiction. | Galapagos tortoises—Fiction. | Turtles—Fiction. | Galapagos Islands—Fiction.
Classification: LCC PZ7.O81167 Tu 2023 (print) | LCC PZ7.O81167 (ebook) |
DDC [Fic]—dc23

Printed in the United States of America
10 9 8 7 6 5 4 3 2 1

This book has been officially leveled by using the F&P Text Level Gradient™ Leveling System.

Random House Children's Books supports the First Amendment and celebrates the right to read.

To

Sophia Jade Futrell

CONTENTS

	Prologue	1
1.	To a Port Far Away	3
2.	Morgan's Magic	11
3.	The Enchanted Islands	20
4.	Flamingo Lagoon	30
5.	Time for Tortoises	37
6.	The Worst News	45
7.	Rivers of Fire	53
8.	The Last One	62
9.	The Turtle King	71
10.	A Lucky Break	81

PROLOGUE

One summer day in Frog Creek, Pennsylvania, a mysterious tree house appeared in the woods. It was filled with books. A boy named Jack and his sister, Annie, found the tree house and soon discovered that it was magic. They could go to any time and place in history just by pointing to a picture in one of the books. While they were gone, no time at all passed back in Frog Creek.

Jack and Annie eventually found out that the tree house belonged to Morgan le Fay, a magical librarian from the legendary realm of Camelot.

Since then, they have traveled on many adventures in the magic tree house and completed many missions for Morgan.

On their most recent adventure, Jack and Annie traveled to South Africa and met heroes working to protect endangered rhinos. Now they're about to head to an amazing island in the Pacific Ocean to meet more heroes who are helping to save other endangered species.

1

To a Port Far Away

Knock, knock.

Jack opened his eyes and looked at his clock.

It said 6:13 a.m.

It was Tuesday, a school day. But school didn't start for another two hours.

Knock, knock.

Why was someone knocking on his door? Jack wondered.

"Come in," he murmured.

The door opened. Annie slipped into the room.

"Guess what," she said in a hushed voice. "You

won't believe it! I saw an albatross flying outside my window!"

"A what?" said Jack.

"An albatross!" said Annie. "A huge white bird that flies over the ocean. It can fly or float on the water for years without ever touching land. And it was circling our house!"

"You're right—I don't believe it," said Jack. He rolled over and closed his eyes.

"No, it was *real.* I promise!" said Annie. "It was a messenger from a faraway place. I'm sure of it. Like that oxpecker bird that only lives in Africa. Remember? It led us to the grasslands."

Jack suddenly felt fully awake. "Oh," he said. He sat up. "Maybe we should check it out."

"Yes! Come on, let's go!" said Annie.

"Okay, but we have to be back in fifteen minutes, before Mom and Dad wake up," said Jack.

"Meet you outside," said Annie.

"Right!" said Jack.

Annie left Jack's room. Jack changed into his jeans, a T-shirt, and a hoodie. Then he slipped down the stairs and met Annie on the front porch.

The morning was gray and chilly. Annie was looking at the early September sky.

"Do you see the white bird?" asked Jack.

"No," said Annie, frowning. "Let's check the woods."

"Okay. But we'd better make it fast," said Jack.

Jack and Annie left their porch. They hurried across the yard and up their street.

"Hey, I see it now!" said Jack. "Oh, man, it's huge!"

The albatross was flying above the Frog Creek woods.

"It has the widest wingspan of any bird on earth!" said Annie.

"It's incredible!" said Jack.

He and Annie dashed across the street and into the woods.

As they ran, a cool breeze made the leaves rustle. Early morning birds were calling out to each other.

Jack and Annie ran between the trees until they came to the tallest oak. They looked up.

"Good work!" said Jack.

The magic tree house *was* back.

"Thank the albatross, not me," said Annie.

The giant white bird was circling high above the tree house. It dipped down for a moment. Then it soared off into the gray sky.

"We're on our way!" Annie called after the albatross.

She and Jack scrambled up the rope ladder. As soon as they were inside the tree house, Jack saw a piece of paper on the floor. He picked it up.

"Morgan's handwriting!" he said. He read aloud:

Your badges are magic.
You'll be what they say.
Clip them on when you land
In a port far away.

Show them to strangers,
And they'll all agree.
No matter your age,
"Experts" they'll see.

But the expert to find,
The one to admire,

Is the one you must save
From a river of fire.

Be honest and gentle.
No need to be smart.
Just look eye to eye
And talk heart to heart.

"Magic badges?" said Annie.

She and Jack looked around the tree house.

"There!" said Jack. He pointed to two badges tucked in a corner.

Annie grabbed them. "They look like name tags," she said, "but they're blank."

Annie handed one of the badges to Jack. It had a clip to attach it to a piece of clothing.

Jack looked at Morgan's rhyme again. "According to this, we put them on when we land. And then we each become an expert."

"But what kind of expert?" said Annie.

"I don't know," said Jack. "It seems we're about to know tons of stuff about something, like you know about animals."

"Oh, I only know a little compared to a real expert," said Annie.

"Then I wonder what kind of real experts we'll be," said Jack. He looked around the tree house. The only book he saw was the Pennsylvania book that always took them home.

"Darn, no research book," Jack said.

"Like our last trip," said Annie.

"Yeah, but at least then we had a little brochure to read," said Jack.

"Oh!" said Annie. "I get it! Morgan said we'd turn into experts. If we're experts, we won't need lots of extra information to help us!"

"Maybe," said Jack. "Okay. Let's go." He looked at Morgan's note again. "I think if we point to the words *a port far away,* the tree house will take us there."

"Wait—what's a port, exactly?" asked Annie.

"You know, a town where ships and other boats go in and out," said Jack. "It's usually beside the sea."

"Oh, right, makes sense," said Annie. "That's where an albatross would hang out, for sure. Let's try it."

Jack pointed to the words *a port far away.*

"I wish we could go *there*!" he said.

The wind started to blow.

The tree house started to spin.

It spun faster and faster.

Then everything was still.

Absolutely still.

2

Morgan's Magic

A soft sea breeze blew into the tree house.

Jack heard birds cawing and waves crashing. He inhaled moist, salty air.

"Nice clothes," said Annie. "We look good."

"Yeah, we do," said Jack. They were both wearing long-sleeved green shirts with pockets, baggy tan cargo pants, and hiking boots.

They looked out the window together. The tree house had landed in a palm tree. The tree stood at the edge of a long white beach. Sunlight sparkled on gentle ocean waves.

"There's the beautiful bird!" said Annie.

An albatross was gliding on the wind. Seagulls and black birds with huge wings also circled above the beach.

Out in the ocean, a motorboat was speeding toward a dock that extended beyond the shoreline.

"Okay. A motorboat," said Jack. "We must not have gone very far into the past."

"I see trucks, too," said Annie. She pointed to two white pickup trucks parked near the beach. "And our clothes. Ready to climb down?"

"Wait. Our badges," said Jack.

"Oh, right," said Annie. She handed Jack his badge.

Jack and Annie clipped the badges to the pockets of their green shirts.

"Ready now," said Jack.

Annie gasped. "Wait! Something's happening to our badges!"

Jack looked at Annie's badge.

One at a time, letters were magically appearing until they spelled:

ANNIE
WORLD TURTLE EXPERT

"World Turtle Expert?" Jack said. He looked down at his own badge. It now said:

JACK
WORLD TURTLE EXPERT

"But what does that mean?" said Jack.

"It means we're World Turtle Experts," said Annie.

"But what does *that* mean?" said Jack.

"It means we're World Turtle Experts!" said Annie again. "Get it?"

"Turtles? . . . Really?" said Jack. He looked out

the window. To his surprise, his mind was suddenly filled with expert turtle information.

"Oh, I know where we are now," he said with wonder. "We landed on Isabela Island. It's part of the Galápagos Islands!"

"Right!" said Annie, looking with him. "The Galápagos belong to the country of Ecuador. Any turtle expert would recognize this place."

"Of course," said Jack. "It's world-famous for having the biggest tortoises in the world—the Galápagos giant tortoises!"

"The kings and queens of the turtle world!" exclaimed Annie. "I love giant tortoises!"

"Who doesn't?" said Jack. "Most of the Galápagos is a national park to protect wildlife. On the islands, you'll find fifteen different—"

Suddenly Jack shook his head. "Wait—wait—this is too weird. Let's take these off." He unclipped his badge from his shirt.

Annie did the same.

"I don't know what I'm saying," said Jack. "I never knew anything about these islands before. I've never even heard of them! And turtles! Really? I never knew anything about turtles."

"Well, we do now—when we wear our badges," said Annie. "Get it? They instantly turned us into turtle experts and gave us a bunch of knowledge." She picked up their note again. "Listen—"

Your badges are magic.
You'll be what they say.
Clip them on when you land
In a port far away.

"But this is too strange," said Jack. "I don't feel like myself. I don't sound like myself."

"I know, but it's fun," said Annie. "I love being a World Turtle Expert. Don't you?"

"I—I don't know . . . ," said Jack.

"Hey, it's just like the time Morgan gave us magic baseball caps, remember?" said Annie. "When we wore them, we instantly became batboys in a major-league game. We knew everything we needed to know."

"Yeah . . . right, we did," said Jack.

Annie read more from the note:

Show them to strangers,
And they'll all agree.
No matter your age,
"Experts" they'll see.

"Wow, this is so incredible," said Annie. "When strangers see our badges, they'll totally believe we're grown-up experts. They won't see us as know-nothing kids."

"How's that possible?" said Jack.

"It's Morgan's magic!" said Annie. "Remember when people saw us wearing the magic baseball caps? They thought we were both teenage boys!"

"Yeah, till a fan stole my cap," said Jack. "Then everyone saw me as a kid lost on the ballfield."

"Right, that was a disaster," said Annie. "Just make sure you don't lose your badge. Keep it clipped to your shirt. Come on, let's go. Let's be World Turtle Experts for a day!"

Jack laughed. "Yeah, okay," he said.

They both clipped their badges back on.

Suddenly Jack began rattling off more information. "On the Galápagos Islands, there are fifteen different kinds of giant tortoises. In fact, there are five kinds on this island alone. They live on—"

"Wait, stop!" said Annie. "You don't need to tell *me*. I know all this information, too! Let's go meet those turtles! Come on!"

3

The Enchanted Islands

Jack tucked Morgan's note into his back pocket. Then he followed Annie down the rope ladder to the beach.

"Head toward the boat dock," said Jack. "We can ask for information there."

As Jack and Annie started walking, their hiking boots made tracks in the white sand. The breeze smelled of salt water and fish.

They walked between pink lizards sunbathing on the beach and seagulls picking at seaweed.

"This place has a ton of wildlife," said Annie.

“Yep. I bet you don’t know that the Galápagos have over nine thousand different types of creatures,” said Jack.

“I know that,” said Annie.

“Right, you’re a World Turtle Expert, too,” he said. “Sorry.”

They skirted around sandpipers running toward the water and birds with big blue feet waddling at the ocean’s edge. They passed a couple of sea lions resting on their backs.

The sea lions lifted their heads to look at Jack and Annie. They seemed to smile.

“Livin’ the dream!” Annie called out to them.

Jack laughed.

“They seem so relaxed and unafraid,” said Annie.

“There’s a reason for that,” said Jack. “For millions of years, the Galápagos Islands were cut off from the rest of the world. So the wildlife here never developed a fear of people.”

"Yes, I know," said Annie.

"That's why explorers used to call the islands *the Enchanted Islands*," Jack went on. "They thought all the creatures were under a spell."

"Yes," said Annie. "I know. In fact—"

Jack interrupted her. "And did you know the islands were created by volcanoes under the ocean? Over millions of years, layers of lava turned into islands."

"Well, yes, Jack, I know," said Annie. "In fact—"

"And," interrupted Jack, "there are still thirteen active volcanoes on these islands. Did you know that?"

"Jack!" said Annie. "We're *both* World Turtle Experts. Everything you know, I know, too!"

"Oh, right," said Jack.

"In fact, today there are *six* active volcanoes here on Isabela Island alone," Annie added.

"Hmm," said Jack. "Maybe we should ask someone about those volcanoes."

"Oh, wow, brown pelicans!" said Annie. "I love pelicans."

Jack and Annie had arrived at the wooden pier that stretched out into the water. A number of brown pelicans hovered near tied-up vessels. An older man with a beard was hauling in a fishing net from his boat.

"Look!" said Annie, pointing. "Tourists."

At the end of the pier, passengers were stepping off the boat Jack and Annie had seen. The writing on the boat said GALÁPAGOS CRUISES.

The tourists wore baggy shorts, flowered shirts, and sun hats. They carried beach bags and cameras.

"Mister! Where are the taxis?" a man bellowed at the fisherman.

The fisherman didn't look at the tourists. He

just pointed to the two white pickup trucks waiting near the beach.

As Jack and Annie stood at the entrance of the pier, Jack held his breath. Would the tourists see him and Annie as World Turtle Experts?

But as the group bustled by, everyone was talking and laughing loudly. They passed Jack and Annie without a glance. A moment later, they were all piling into the white trucks by the shore.

"Okay. Let's go talk to that fisherman," said Jack. "We'll find out if *he* sees us as experts."

"Good idea," said Annie. "We'll ask him about the turtles."

"Yeah, and we can ask about the six active volcanoes here on Isabela Island," said Jack.

As Jack and Annie started down the pier, their hiking boots thumped over the worn wooden planks.

"Hi, guys!" Annie called out to a couple of pelicans perched on the railing. Suddenly one swooped up into the air and stole a small fish from a seagull.

"Whoa! Not fair!" Annie shouted at the funny-looking bird.

The pelican landed on the railing, threw back its head, and swallowed the fish whole.

Jack and Annie both laughed.

"Listen to me," Annie said to the pelican. "Don't take what doesn't belong to you."

The pelican lowered its head.

"Good. You *should* be embarrassed," Annie said.

Jack laughed again. "Annie, don't forget, when we meet people, you can't treat wildlife like they're human," he said. "Experts don't do that."

"Oh, right," said Annie. "I guess I just slipped back into my real self."

She and Jack kept walking toward the fisherman.

"Hello!" Jack called out.

The man didn't turn around. "Don't worry. More tourist taxis coming soon," he said in a grumpy voice.

"Actually, we're not tourists," said Annie.

The fisherman looked over his shoulder.

Jack and Annie pointed to their badges.

The fisherman seemed startled. "Oh, I see!" he said. "You're World Turtle Experts. My mistake."

The magic works! thought Jack.

"Are you from the National Park Service?" the fisherman asked.

"No, we've just come from America to study Galápagos turtles," said Annie.

"Can you tell us the best spot to do that?" asked Jack.

"You need to talk to the people at the Giant Tortoise Center," the man said.

"Sounds good," said Jack. "How do we get there?"

"If you're walking, just head toward town," said the fisherman. "Take the Wildlife Trail off the main road. Follow the boardwalk through Flamingo Lagoon. And you'll come right to the center."

"Great! Thanks!" said Annie.

As they started away, Annie grabbed Jack's arm. "The magic works!" she whispered.

"I know, I know," said Jack. "Wait. . . ." He

called back to the fisherman. "Excuse me, sir, one more question! What's the volcano activity these days?"

The fisherman frowned and shook his head.

"Not good?" said Jack.

"The Blue Hill volcano erupted two weeks ago," the man said. "The lava is still flowing."

"Oh, wow, where is that?" asked Annie.

"About thirty-five miles from here," the fisherman said.

"Oh, good. It's far away," said Annie.

"So I guess that means we're safe?" said Jack.

"Completely," the man said.

"Thanks for your help!" said Annie.

"Have a nice day!" said Jack.

As they walked back down the dock, Jack smiled. "That's good," he said. "For once, we're not in danger."

4

Flamingo Lagoon

Jack and Annie stepped off the pier. They walked up a sandy road into a small town.

They passed a few small shops: Seaside Gifts, the Green Lizard, the Tortoise Tavern.

"This isn't much of a town," said Jack. "It seems pretty empty."

"Maybe the active volcano is keeping most tourists away," said Annie.

"That's silly," said Jack. "The fisherman said it's completely safe here."

"True," said Annie. "But bad news can scare people."

"Stop," said Jack. He pointed at a sign marked WILDLIFE TRAIL. "There's the path that the fisherman told us to look for."

He and Annie left the road. They walked down a pebble path shaded by tree branches.

"Oh, wow! A pink iguana!" said Annie.

They stopped to look at a huge lizard resting on a branch. The iguana had pale pink skin with dark stripes.

"It looks like a tiny dinosaur," said Annie.

"The Galápagos are the only place on Earth where pink iguanas live," said Jack. "They've been here about five million years."

"I know," said Annie.

"Come on, there's the boardwalk over the lagoon," said Jack.

He and Annie headed over the raised wooden

walkway. As they crossed the murky water, they saw even more wildlife.

The dark pond was filled with ducks. Birds were cheeping and flitting everywhere.

"Mockingbirds, finches," Jack said.

"Herons and flamingos!" said Annie.

Blue herons stood in the shallows. A pair of flamingos waded together with slow, graceful steps. They dipped their heads into the water.

"They're like dancers taking a bow!" Annie said. She jumped up and down and clapped her hands. "Yay!" she shouted.

"Annie, you need to calm down," said Jack. "If you want people to see you as an expert, you can't act like a kid."

"Right, sorry," said Annie.

Jack and Annie left the boardwalk. They followed a short trail through a dry, mossy forest. The air smelled of mint.

Bright-yellow iguanas and long green lizards rested on tree trunks and branches. The whole island seemed alive with amazing creatures.

The forest soon opened into a clearing.

A one-story wooden building was bathed in sunlight. It had a thatched roof and a yard with fencing.

A sign said: GIANT TORTOISE CENTER.

"That's it!" said Annie. "A turtle expert's dream!"

"Right, but when we go inside, remember that experts act cool," said Jack.

"Cool is boring," murmured Annie.

"Yeah, but knowledge isn't," said Jack. "And we have tons of it."

As they walked up to the entrance, two white pickup trucks rolled into a parking area near the center.

"Oh, brother, it's the tourists from the Galápagos Cruises boat," Jack said.

"What's wrong with that?" asked Annie.

"I just hope they don't get in our way," Jack said.

"Don't worry," said Annie. "We don't even know what we're supposed to do yet."

Jack and Annie stepped into the lobby of the Giant Tortoise Center.

The lobby was filled with wildlife displays and a map of the building and grounds.

A tall young woman with a long black ponytail stood at a counter. She wore a green uniform and was quickly making notes as she talked to someone on the phone.

"Yes, sir, I understand," she said. "Emergency action was taken earlier today. But now they must try again."

What emergency action? Jack wondered.

The woman glanced up and saw Jack and Annie.

They both pointed to their name badges.

The woman's eyes grew wide. "I have to call you right back," she said into the phone. Then she hung up.

"Welcome, Jack and Annie!" she said. "I'm Carmen, the only guide at the center right now. No one told me important guests were coming today. Our director should have been here to greet you. But we have an emergency—"

Before Carmen could finish, the tourist group from the boat banged through the front door.

5

Time for Tortoises

Jack wanted to ask Carmen about the emergency. But the tourists immediately started asking questions.

"Excuse me, do we have to pay?"

"Do you have a bathroom here?"

"We brought boxed lunches—where can we eat at lunchtime?"

"I'll answer all your questions in a minute," Carmen assured them. "But first, I need to speak to our special guests."

She turned back to Jack and Annie. "As I was

saying, our director isn't here because of a crisis. I want to show you around the center. But I need to make some calls first."

"Carmen, don't worry about us," Annie said firmly. "How can we help *you*?"

"Goodness, you're so kind. Could you"—Carmen looked at the noisy tourists—"could you give them information about the center and the tortoises, please?"

"Of course," said Annie. "We can handle that."

"No problem," said Jack.

"Oh, thank you!" said Carmen. She pointed to the map on the wall. "That shows you the layout of our center. Perhaps you can lead them around while I deal with this crisis."

"Could you tell us about the crisis?" Jack asked, trying to sound like an expert.

"Yes," said Carmen. "The Park Service called about more endangered turtles and—"

"Miss! Miss!" a man interrupted Carmen. "Can you just tell all of us how to find the tortoises?"

"No, I can't tell you—I need to show you," said Carmen, sounding upset. "Sorry." She seemed flustered. "Jack, Annie, could you please—"

"Go ahead, Carmen. We got this," said Annie.

"Make your calls," said Jack.

"Oh, you're lifesavers! Thank you!" said Carmen. And she slipped into a back room.

"I'll look at the map," Jack said to Annie. "You get their attention." He hurried over to the map on the wall.

"Greetings, friends!" Annie called out.

No one seemed to hear her. Noise from the chattering tourists filled the lobby.

"GREETINGS, FRIENDS!" Jack shouted. He pointed at his badge for all to see.

The tourists looked startled. A couple of them loudly shushed the others. "SHHH! SHHH!"

"Thank you," said Annie. "And welcome to the Giant Tortoise Center. I'm Annie—and that's my brother, Jack." She pointed at Jack, studying the map. "We are your World Turtle Experts today."

People spoke softly to each other:

"World Turtle Experts?"

"That's a big deal."

"I'm so impressed."

Jack returned to Annie's side. "First, there are some rules to follow," he said to the group. "Rule number one: Please do not talk or laugh loudly. Our tortoise friends prefer peaceful surroundings."

"Rule two: Please do not touch any tortoises," said Annie. "And rule three: Please don't take photos of them. This is their home and we are their guests."

Everyone nodded meekly.

"Thank you for your cooperation," said Jack. "Okay! Now follow us."

Jack and Annie led the tourists out of the lobby and down a hall. They stopped in front of a closed door.

"Let's pause for a moment," Jack said. "We're about to enter an area with many giant tortoises."

The group murmured with excitement.

"But none of these tortoises are really giant . . . yet," said Annie. "You are about to meet many tiny turtle babies and little turtle kids."

"Hatchlings," said Jack. "The name for a baby turtle is *hatchling.*"

"Hold on there," said a large bald man. "You

say *tortoises* one moment and *turtles* the next. Which are they?"

"Excellent question," said Jack.

"Yes, we World Turtle Experts get that question a lot," said Annie.

"All tortoises are turtles," said Jack. "But not all turtles are tortoises. The giant tortoises of the Galápagos are the largest members of the turtle family."

"Think of them as the kings and queens of the turtle world!" said Annie.

"Oh! I *love* giant tortoises!" said a woman in a sun hat.

"Me too!" said Annie.

"And the Galápagos Islands need them," said Jack. "Tortoises are vital to the ecosystem here and—"

"Can you explain that?" interrupted the large man.

"Sure. An ecosystem is a biological community

of interacting organisms and their physical environment," Jack explained.

No one said anything. They all looked confused.

Annie stepped in. "Jack means that everything on this island is connected. Tortoises, trees, other plants, insects—all work together. If you destroy one of them, you harm the others. Understand?"

The tourists nodded with serious looks.

"A few hundred years ago, pirates and whale hunters visited these islands," said Jack. "They

killed hundreds of thousands of giant tortoises for food."

"Oh, no! I hate that," said a woman with curly red hair.

"I could cry!" said the woman in the sun hat.

"Me too," said Annie.

"We all could," said Jack. "But fortunately, things have changed. Today, the National Park Service is doing all it can to help the giant tortoises live long, happy lives."

"Hurray for them!" exclaimed the woman with curly red hair.

"*Mom, quiet,*" whispered a teenage girl.

"Yes, hurray for them!" said Annie.

"There are good people everywhere trying to help endangered animals," said Jack. "Are you ready?"

Everyone nodded.

"Time for tortoises!" Annie said. And she opened the door to the outside.

6

The Worst News

The group followed Jack and Annie into the fenced yard.

"We'll visit the hatchery first," said Jack.

He led everyone to a row of wooden trays covered with screens. Annie removed one of the screens.

"OH, WOW!" she said.

"Annie," said Jack.

"Sorry," she whispered. She lowered her voice. "Everyone, please step closer and have a good look."

The tourists moved forward. They murmured with excitement.

The tray was filled with eggs the size of tennis balls. Tiny tortoises crawled among some of the eggs.

Jack picked up an egg. “Park Service workers collect tortoise eggs in the wild,” he said. “They bring them here to keep them safe.”

Annie lifted a tiny tortoise from the tray. She set it in the palm of her hand. “A newly hatched giant,” she said.

“Aww! I could die!” said the red-haired woman.

“Me too,” said Annie. “This tiny baby is only three inches long and weighs only a few ounces. But get this—it will grow to be a thousand times bigger! As an adult, it could easily weigh more than five hundred pounds!”

The group gasped.

“Some baby!” laughed an old man.

“I know. It’s a miracle, isn’t it?” said Annie.

The tiny tortoise stretched out its neck and turned its head.

"It looks positively ancient," said the red-haired woman.

"In a way, it is," said Jack. "Giant tortoises have lived on the Galápagos for two or three million years."

"Good luck, sweetie!" Annie said softly to the tiny tortoise. "Have a nice life." And she carefully returned the hatchling to the tray.

"So when that hatchling is older, it will be moved over here," said Jack. He led the group to an open pen.

The tourists gasped with wonder.

Hundreds of small tortoises were crawling around in grass and dirt. Some were munching green stalks. Others were climbing rocks or soaking in pools of water.

The tourists whispered and smiled.

"Do they have any brains?" the old man asked.

"You mean are they smart?" said Annie.

"Yes, they are," answered Jack. "Tortoises are super-smart. They have a different kind of brainpower than we have. But they know exactly how to live their lives."

"And those lives are really *long*," said Annie. "Tortoises can live for more than one hundred fifty years."

"Whoa!" said the old man with a laugh. "What's their secret?"

"Another excellent question," said Annie. "Besides having a shell that protects them, their secret is living a quiet, peaceful life. They never hurry. They spend their days resting in the sunlight, eating plants, and soaking in puddles."

"Sounds good to me!" the old man roared.

"I heard tortoises are deaf," the red-haired woman said.

"That's not exactly true," said Jack. "They don't hear well, but they can feel vibrations."

"How do you know if one is male or female?" asked the woman in the sun hat.

"When it's fully grown, you can tell by its belly," said Jack. "If the belly curves inward, it's a male. Now, Annie, why don't you tell our friends about releasing the tortoises into the wild?"

"When the tortoises are about five years old, they are ready to live on their own," said Annie. "At that age, they're about the size of a melon."

"What kind of melon?" the old man asked.

"Hmm . . . maybe a honeydew?" said Annie.

Suddenly the door to the center opened. Carmen stepped into the yard. "Jack, Annie!" she called. "May I have a quick word?"

"Excuse us," Jack said to the group. He and Annie rushed over to Carmen.

"The Park Service needs your help right away," Carmen said in a hushed voice.

"What is it?" said Jack.

"Special Forces will explain," said Carmen. "They're waiting outside the front door. You go. I'll take care of the visitors."

Carmen hurried to the tortoise pen, and Jack and Annie slipped back into the building.

As they headed to the lobby, Jack's heart was pounding. "Special Forces? This must be the emergency Carmen was talking about," he said. "I wonder what is going on!"

"I don't know," said Annie. "But it can't be good."

When they went out the front door of the center, Jack and Annie saw two strong-looking men standing near a white pickup truck. Their backs were toward Jack and Annie. They were dressed in green military uniforms.

"Point to your badge," Annie said to Jack.

"Right," said Jack.

Pointing to their World Turtle Expert badges, Jack and Annie headed over to the soldiers.

"Excuse us, gentlemen," said Annie.

Both soldiers turned around. When they saw the badges, they both saluted Jack and Annie.

"Very glad you're here, Jack and Annie. I'm Captain Cruz," said one of the men.

"Captain Pinto," said the other. "Ecuadorian Special Forces."

"What's up, Captain?" Jack asked calmly.

"Rescue mission on Blue Hill volcano," said Pinto. "National Park Service asked for our help."

"All giant tortoises are being cleared from a small area of the volcano," Cruz said. "A fiery river of molten lava is heading their way."

"Oh, dear," said Annie.

"We assume you're familiar with this sort of tortoise rescue mission," Cruz said.

"Yes, sir. No problem," said Annie.

Jack barely nodded. As a World Turtle Expert, he knew all about tortoises but nothing about how to deal with fiery rivers of molten lava!

"Good. Let's go," said Cruz.

"On it," said Annie. She followed Pinto and Cruz to yet another white pickup truck. She looked back. "Jack?"

Jack took a deep breath. "Yep. On it," he murmured. And he hurried after Annie and the soldiers.

7

Rivers of Fire

The two soldiers climbed into the front of the truck. Jack and Annie sat in back.

Cruz started the engine. The truck turned onto a back road. Then it sped away from the Giant Tortoise Center.

Annie looked at Jack. "We've got this," she said in a low voice.

Jack wasn't so sure. He leaned forward. "Sirs, can you explain *our* part in this mission?" he said.

"A small group of giant tortoises live on the

southwest side of the Blue Hill volcano. We thought they were safe," said Pinto. "Until yesterday."

"What happened yesterday?" asked Jack.

"The lava river split into two streams," said Pinto. "One of them is now flowing toward the home ground of the Blue Hill tortoises."

Annie nodded. "That's bad," she said.

"Yes, but there were earlier airlifts today," said Cruz. "Hopefully, our team has rescued them all."

"But there could be stragglers," said Pinto.

"And this is the last chance to help them escape," said Cruz.

Jack's expert self was very alarmed. "Gentlemen, it's absolutely vital we save every last one," he said. "The tortoises of Blue Hill are extremely rare. Reports say ninety-eight percent of their population has disappeared in the last one hundred eighty years. We can't afford to lose any of them."

“Understood,” said Pinto.

Jack sat back in his seat and took a deep breath. Right now, his fear for the tortoises was greater than any fear of an active volcano.

He nodded to Annie. “We’ve got this,” he said.

“Read Morgan’s rhyme,” she whispered.

“Why?” asked Jack. As an expert, he’d given little thought to Morgan’s rhyme. He hadn’t felt they’d needed it.

“To make sure we’re doing the right thing,” said Annie.

“We are,” said Jack confidently. But just to please Annie, he pulled out the rhyme. As they read it together, Annie pointed to the third section:

But the expert to find,
The one to admire,
Is the one you must save
From a river of fire.

"No problem," Jack said in her ear. "Morgan's talking about the giant tortoises. They're obviously the true experts. They're the experts at being giant tortoises. It's all falling into place."

"Right. But read *this* part," said Annie. She pointed to the last section. Jack read to himself:

Be honest and gentle.
No need to be smart.
Just look eye to eye
And talk heart to heart.

"That's super-important," Annie whispered to Jack.

Jack nodded. Those lines were nice. But as an expert, he certainly didn't find them "super-important."

He tucked the rhyme back into his pocket.

The truck headed along the road beside the

ocean and passed the few shops. Then it bounced over a long sandy road.

The road ended at a small airstrip. A military helicopter was waiting.

"There's our chopper," said Cruz.

"A chopper ride! Wow!" said Annie. "That's our first—"

Jack held up his hand to stop her.

"That's our *favorite* way to travel," Annie said, correcting herself.

Cruz parked near the runway. "It will get us there quickly. We'll be on the volcano in ten or fifteen minutes."

"Good. The sooner the better," said Jack. His expert self was unafraid of taking his first chopper ride.

The four of them climbed out of the truck and hurried to the runway. The helicopter's cockpit had four seats.

Jack and Annie climbed into the seats behind the two pilots. Cruz handed them helmets, and they strapped them on.

"How does this chopper transport tortoises?" Jack asked.

"We have crates in the cargo section," said Cruz.

A moment later, the blades started to swirl.

With a roar, the helicopter lifted off the ground. It rocked from side to side, then headed into the sky.

Annie grinned at Jack. "Yikes!" she mouthed.

Jack gave her a thumbs-up.

The helicopter flew over flat, rocky land dotted with bushes and other plants.

Pinto pointed to a distant dome-shaped volcano with sloping sides. "That's it!" he shouted above the roar of the chopper blades.

A cloud of steam rose from the top of Blue Hill.

Red-hot lava bubbled down the sides.

"WHOA!" said Annie.

Jack tapped his finger against his mouth, reminding her to act cool. But his heart pounded as the chopper drew closer.

The volcanic eruption looked terrifying. Jack could see the two fiery streams that had split from the lava river. Lava was also oozing from cracks in the slope. Patches of grass were catching fire. Smoke filled the air.

The helicopter started to land on a lower part of the volcano. The surface was rough and craggy from ancient lava flows.

Through the smoke, Jack saw black rocks of all sizes, tall grass, and thick clumps of bright-yellow and apple-green cactus plants.

"Good tortoise food—prickly pear cactus," Jack shouted to Pinto and Cruz.

"They like the yellow lava cactus, too," shouted

Annie. "It only grows on the volcanoes of the Galápagos."

"That's where we should begin our search!" shouted Jack.

"Understood," shouted Pinto.

The spinning blades were slowing as the helicopter settled on the slope. Finally they came to a full stop.

“Okay! Let’s go!” said Cruz. “Make it fast! That lava will be here before we know it!”

“Understood!” said Annie. She and Jack took off their helmets and climbed down onto the rough black ground.

8

THE LAST ONE

The smoky air was hot and steamy.

Above Jack and Annie, the stream of liquid fire was steadily moving their way.

"Separate and search the area!" said Cruz.

Jack, Annie, Cruz, and Pinto headed in different directions to search for giant tortoises still stranded on the volcano.

As Jack stepped around chunks of jagged black rock, his eyes and throat burned from the smoke.

He moved between thickets of green prickly

pear cactus and lava cactus. He bent down to look behind a lava plant.

"Ouch!" he yelped.

The lava cactus had needle-sharp spines. A clump of spines had poked through his shirt sleeve, pricking his skin.

Jack yanked his arm loose, nearly falling over.

"All clear!" Cruz shouted. "Annie?"

"Clear, sir!" shouted Annie.

"Jack?" shouted Cruz.

"Clear!" Jack yelled hoarsely.

But suddenly nothing seemed clear. He could hardly see through the smoke. His thoughts were muddled. His arm hurt. He didn't know what he was doing.

"We have to move quick! The lava will be here soon!" Cruz yelled. "Meet you at the chopper."

Jack stumbled away from the cactus plants. He

looked up and saw the river of lava oozing down the slope. He felt terrified.

"Let's go, Jack!" Annie called.

Jack didn't answer.

"Jack, are you okay?" Annie called, running to him.

"No! Yes!" said Jack, breathing hard. "I don't know!"

"Hey! Where's your badge?" cried Annie.

Jack looked down at his shirt. "Oh, no! It's gone!" he said. "It must have come unclipped from my pocket!" He looked around wildly.

"Okay. Stay calm. Don't panic," said Annie.

"But Cruz and Pinto will see I'm just a kid!"

cried Jack. "It's happened again! Just like when I lost my magic baseball cap!"

"Don't worry—we'll find it. You start looking," said Annie. "I'll go tell the guys you have one more place to search for tortoises."

Annie took off. Jack started crawling on his hands and knees, frantically searching for his badge.

He crawled around the prickly pear and lava cactus.

He looked deep into crevices.

He peered under a shelf of rock.

He gasped.

Two shining eyes stared back at him.

Jack scrunched down to see better.

The shiny black eyes belonged to a giant tortoise!

"Oh, no!" Jack said. "We can't be here! You have to go! Lava's coming this way!"

The creature kept staring at Jack with a calm,

thoughtful gaze. The tortoise was completely tucked inside the small cave of rock. There was no way to get it out.

Jack wished he were wearing his badge! He didn't know anything about giant tortoises now—how to help them or what to do! He was overcome with fear and confusion.

"You've got to come out!" Jack begged. "Please. . . . Annie!" he called, but his voice was hoarse. "Annie!"

"Listen! Lava's coming!" Jack said to the tortoise. "It's burning up everything in its path!"

The creature still didn't move.

"Oh, come out! Please! Hurry!" Jack pleaded. He put all his heart into begging the tortoise. "Please! Lava's headed this way! You'll be killed if you don't come out. There are soldiers to fly you to safety. Please, start walking! Walk to me, and I can take you to them! You're—you're one of the last of your kind. . . . You—you have to come out. . . ." Jack felt tears in his eyes. "We can't lose you. Please."

Slowly, finally, the tortoise stuck out its neck. It started toward Jack on its thick, stumpy legs.

"Yes! Oh, man, that's it! Keep coming, keep coming!" Jack urged. He crawled backward to make room for the tortoise. "Faster. Walk faster."

The giant tortoise kept plodding forward until it stepped out from under the ledge.

The creature's small head moved close to Jack's face. Its flat nose was almost touching Jack's nose.

Jack held his breath as he looked straight into the bright black eyes of the giant tortoise. He and the tortoise stared at each other for a long moment. Jack felt as if he were looking into a face as old as time. He felt as if the two of them had known each other forever.

"You're going to be okay," he whispered to the tortoise. "I promise. I love you. The whole world loves you."

"Jack! Jack!" Annie called from nearby.

"I'm here!" Jack shouted. "Come quick!"

"Good news!" Annie shouted. "I found your badge! It had fallen between some lava plants! Come on! We're leaving!"

"No! *You* come *here*!" yelled Jack.

Annie hurried around the rocks. "Okay, but what could be better—" Annie stopped short when she saw Jack and the tortoise.

"Oh, wow! You found one! A giant tortoise! I don't believe it!" she cried. "I'll get the guys!"

Annie tossed the badge into the grass near Jack. Then she ran back to the helicopter.

Jack rubbed his finger along the wrinkled, leathery skin of the creature's neck.

"Pinto and Cruz are coming for you now," he said gently to the tortoise. "They'll pick you up. But don't worry. They're super-strong. They're part of Special Forces in Ecuador. They'll fly you to safety."

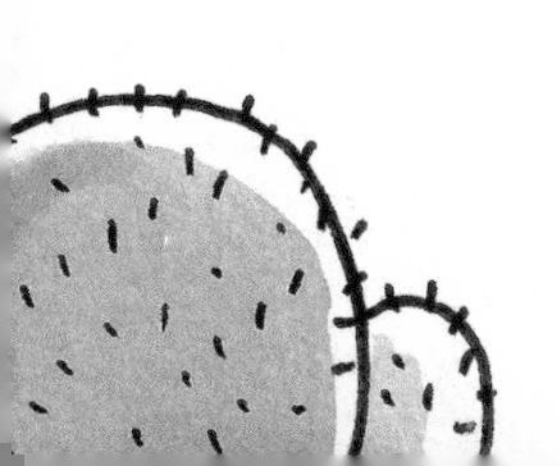

The creature kept looking at Jack with bright, trusting eyes. Its mouth curved into a thin, crooked smile.

Jack smiled back. They kept smiling silently at each other until Jack heard Annie and the soldiers.

Jack grabbed his badge from the grass. He clipped it to his shirt pocket. And instantly, he was a World Turtle Expert again.

9

The Turtle King

"Over here, team!" Jack shouted.

He rose to his feet as Annie and the soldiers raced around the rocks.

"I found the last tortoise," he said. "It was hiding under a ledge."

"Excellent! Good work!" said Cruz. "Pinto and I can carry it to the chopper. But we have to hurry! We're running out of time!"

"Okay. But go easy," said Jack. "I'm guessing it's at least one hundred fifty years old. The shell is softer than you'd think. It's made of honeycomb structures. Very strong, but not rigid."

"Understood," said Pinto.

He and Cruz gripped the big, round shell. Then, very carefully, they lifted the giant tortoise off the ground.

"Ah!" said Jack. "He's a male. His belly curves inward."

"So he's a *king*," Annie murmured to Jack.

"I know," said Jack. "A great king."

"Let's grab some grass for his crate," said Annie.

"Go slow and low," Jack instructed the soldiers. "We'll gather some natural bedding. Meet you at the chopper."

Annie and Jack pulled handfuls of tall grass from the scrubby ground. They hurried through the smoke to the helicopter, opened a side door, and climbed into the cargo area.

Jack and Annie spread the grass on the bottom of a crate.

"A bed fit for a king!" said Annie.

"Yep. He deserves the best," said Jack.

The soldiers carried the giant tortoise to the cargo section. They lifted the creature and carefully placed him in the crate. Then they strapped him inside to keep him safe for the flight.

Pinto made a call from the helicopter phone. Cruz wrote notes on a clipboard.

While the soldiers were busy, Jack and Annie looked at the tortoise.

The turtle king peered back at them. His head bobbed up and down.

"That movement means he's relaxed," said Annie.

"I know," said Jack. "He trusts us."

The tortoise lowered his head, resting it on the soft grass in his crate. He closed his eyes.

"I know what he's thinking," said Jack.

"Really? You do?" said Annie.

"He's thinking, *I'll take a little nap until this part is over,*" said Jack. *"Then I'll be in a safe place. I'll sit in the sun. And they'll give me something good to eat."*

Annie laughed. "You know him pretty well," she said.

"Hurry!" shouted Cruz. "Climb inside! The lava's almost here!" The soldier closed the door to the cargo section.

Jack and Annie scrambled into their seats and put their helmets on.

"Okay! All set!" said Pinto, hanging up the phone. "We have permission to fly him to the Tortoise Center."

The rotor blades started to spin.

With a loud roaring and chopping sound, the helicopter lifted off Blue Hill. It carried them all away from the river of molten lava.

The helicopter flew over the broad slope of the volcano.

It flew over rugged flatlands with patches of green.

It flew along the coastline and over the lagoon.

Finally the helicopter hovered above the grounds of the Giant Tortoise Center.

Jack saw the tourists below. They were sitting in the grass, eating boxed lunches. As the helicopter started to land, they held on to their hats and scurried out of the way, leaving their lunches behind.

The chopper blades finally slowed to a stop. The soldiers, Jack, and Annie jumped out.

Carmen rushed forward to greet them.

"We saved the last one!" Annie said. "He's in the back!"

Carmen burst into tears. She hugged Annie and Jack.

"Thank you!" she said, wiping her eyes. "Thank you so much."

Pinto opened the cargo section.

By now, the tourists were clamoring around the helicopter.

They craned their necks to see the giant tortoise inside.

"No photos of him," Annie reminded them.

"And please keep your voices down," said Jack.

The soldiers lifted the heavy creature out of the crate.

They lowered him to the ground.

Everyone clapped.

Jack held up his hand and tapped his finger on his lips. The tourists quickly stopped making noise.

The tortoise stretched out his neck. He slowly moved his head from side to side. Again, his mouth formed the shape of a crooked smile.

Some tourists laughed quietly. The red-haired woman started to cry. Her daughter wept, too.

"Carmen told us what you were doing!" the red-haired woman said to Jack and Annie. "We've all been so worried!"

"Great job, great job," the large man said in a soft voice.

"You guys rock," said the teenage girl, sniffling.

"How did you land the chopper on a volcano?" the old man asked Cruz.

"How much lava was there?" asked the woman in the sun hat.

The soldiers started answering the tourists' questions about the rescue mission.

Carmen turned to Jack and Annie. "I can't thank you enough," she said. "I'm sure everyone at the National Park Service is grateful for your heroism. We try night and day to care for these miraculous creatures."

"We know," said Annie. "That's why we can't thank *you* enough for the work *you* do. And Pinto and Cruz, too."

"Oh, yes, I must go congratulate them," said Carmen.

She joined the others gathered around the soldiers. By now, the teenage girl was laughing and chatting with Pinto.

"Let's go tell the king good-bye," said Annie.

Jack took a deep breath. "Right," he said.

He and Annie slipped over to the tortoise. They knelt down.

Jack looked into the creature's shining black eyes.

"You're in good hands now," Jack said softly. "Don't worry. One day, your home will be safe again. And you can go back to Blue Hill, where you've lived for one hundred fifty years."

"But for now, just try to enjoy yourself," said Annie. "Think of this as a vacation, Your Majesty. With nice people who love you."

"And remember," said Jack. "You're very brave. You're very wise. You know exactly how to be a giant tortoise. In fact, *you* are the real World Turtle Expert."

The tortoise blinked. Again, he looked as if he were smiling.

"Good-bye," Jack whispered. "We have to go now."

A few tourists wandered over to the tortoise, and Jack and Annie backed away.

To his surprise, Jack felt close to tears again.

"Let's go," he said.

"Thanks, guys! Bye!" Annie yelled to Pinto and Cruz. She held up her two thumbs.

The Special Forces soldiers saluted them.

"Bye, Carmen!" yelled Annie. "Pleasure working with you! If you need further assistance, just—"

"Go, go!" Jack said, giving Annie a nudge.

Without another word, they gave a final wave and hurried away from the Giant Tortoise Center.

10

A Lucky Break

Jack and Annie headed back into the dry, mossy forest.

They hurried past bright-yellow iguanas and long green lizards. They walked over the boardwalk and through the lagoon with flamingos and herons.

They hurried under the archway of trees and into the small town. They passed the shops and stepped onto the beach.

They passed the boat dock and the brown pelicans and started down the shore.

Jack and Annie zigzagged around all the friendly, fearless creatures—sea lions and sandpipers, birds with blue feet, gulls picking at seaweed, and pink lizards sunning in the sand.

Finally they came to their palm tree. They climbed up the rope ladder and into the tree house.

"We made it," said Jack.

"We did," Annie said breathlessly. "We can take these off now." She pulled off her World Turtle Expert badge.

Jack took his off, too. He breathed a sigh of relief. He didn't feel nearly as smart, but he felt happy.

"Can you believe what happened today?" said Annie, grinning. "Everyone thought we were turtle experts!"

"Everyone except the turtle king," said Jack. "He saw my real self."

"I know he did," Annie said. She smiled. "Ready to go?"

"Yep." Jack grabbed the Pennsylvania book.

Together, he and Annie looked out the tree house window.

The huge albatross was circling in the blue sky.

"Good-bye!" Annie shouted to the bird. "Thanks for bringing us to the Enchanted Islands!"

Jack found the photo of Frog Creek and pointed to it.

"I wish we could go there," he said.

The wind started to blow.

The tree house started to spin.

It spun faster and faster.

Then everything was still.

Absolutely still.

The gray early-morning air was chilly.

Jack and Annie were wearing their own clothes again.

A breeze shook the leaves of the oak tree.

While they'd been gone, no time at all had passed in Frog Creek.

"That was fun," said Annie.

Jack smiled and nodded.

But their trip to the Galápagos had been more than just fun, he thought. He'd never forget his moment alone with the giant tortoise. He didn't have words for it.

Annie seemed to guess his thoughts.

"You did a good job," said Annie. "You saved him."

"We all did," said Jack.

"But you did something special. You got him to trust you," said Annie.

"I don't know how. I wasn't an expert when I found him," said Jack. "Without my badge, I felt really scared and confused."

"I know, but losing your badge was a very lucky break," said Annie.

"Why 'lucky'?" asked Jack.

"If you hadn't been looking for it, you wouldn't have found him," said Annie.

"Oh, okay. That's true," said Jack.

"There's more," said Annie. "Do you still have the note from Morgan?"

Jack checked his back pocket.

"Yep, it's here," he said. He handed the note to Annie.

She read the last four lines to him:

Be honest and gentle.
No need to be smart.
Just look eye to eye
And talk heart to heart.

"See. You did just what Morgan wanted," said Annie. "To get to the volcano, we had to be World Turtle Experts."

"Yeah, our knowledge put us in the right

place at the right time," said Jack. "And it helped Pinto and Cruz land in the right spot on the volcano."

"Exactly," said Annie. "But in the most important moment, you were *not* an expert. You were just yourself. Without even thinking of Morgan's rhyme, you spoke to the giant tortoise from your heart. And the heart of the tortoise heard you. And he came out from his hiding place."

Jack nodded. He remembered the creature's brilliant black eyes, his sweet crooked smile. "I guess you're right," he said softly. "I guess you could say we trusted each other."

"Yes. I could say that," said Annie.

"I'll never forget him," said Jack.

"He won't forget you, either," said Annie.

Tears came to Jack's eyes again. He quickly wiped them away.

"Hey—" Annie put her hand on his shoulder. "It's okay to cry," she said.

Jack shook his head. “Experts don’t cry,” he said.

“Sometimes they do,” said Annie.

Jack barely nodded.

“Like right now, I’ll bet experts are crying all across America,” said Annie.

Jack couldn’t help laughing. “Okay. Let’s go,” he said, standing up. “We have to hurry.”

“Yeah, we have to eat breakfast before school,” said Annie, following him. “I’m starving!”

“Me too,” said Jack. He started down the

ladder. Annie followed him, and they walked quickly through the woods.

"We'll wake Mom and Dad up," said Annie. "And we'll say, 'Good morning! We love you! Now please go make us some pancakes!'"

"With blueberries," said Jack.

"Bananas and walnuts," said Annie, stepping off the ladder.

"With maple syrup," said Jack.

"With everything!" said Annie.

And in the early September light, Jack and Annie ran toward home.

A NOTE FROM THE AUTHOR

This book was inspired by an incident that happened in September 1998. The Blue Hill volcano (*Cerro Azul* in Spanish) erupted on Isabela Island in the Galápagos. The rare giant tortoises who lived on the volcano were in deadly danger from the fiery rivers of lava flowing from its crater.

The tortoises were airlifted to safety by helicopter, thanks to the armed forces of Ecuador and workers from Galápagos National Park and the civil defense.

Learn more about turtles and tortoises in

Magic Tree House® Fact Tracker
Snakes and Other Reptiles

Turn the page for a sneak peek!

Eggs on the Beach

Once a year, people see an amazing sight on beaches around the world. Hundreds of female sea turtles crawl up on shore on moonless nights. They use their flippers to dig holes in the sand and lay their eggs. Turtles return to the same beach where they were hatched. When they finish digging and laying their eggs, the turtles crawl slowly back into the sea. About fifty days later, the eggs hatch. Guided by light reflected from the water, the babies head straight for the ocean.

All turtles lay eggs. They usually bury them in the ground or in leaves and brush. Most female turtles leave the nests right after they lay their eggs. Turtle eggs are often at risk. Birds, skunks, and snakes eat them. People do as well.

Sea turtles can lay as many as 150 eggs at a time. Only a few survive.

Food

Many turtles are *omnivores*. This means they eat plants as well as insects and small animals. Snapping turtles gobble up water plants, birds, fish, snakes, and just about anything else they can find, including dead animals. They have very wide throats and swallow big hunks of food.

Some turtles, like green sea turtles and tortoises, are strictly vegetarian. Other sea turtles eat shrimp, crabs, fish, clams, and even jellyfish.

Galápagos tortoises eat a lot of plants. They have to. Some weigh over 500 pounds!

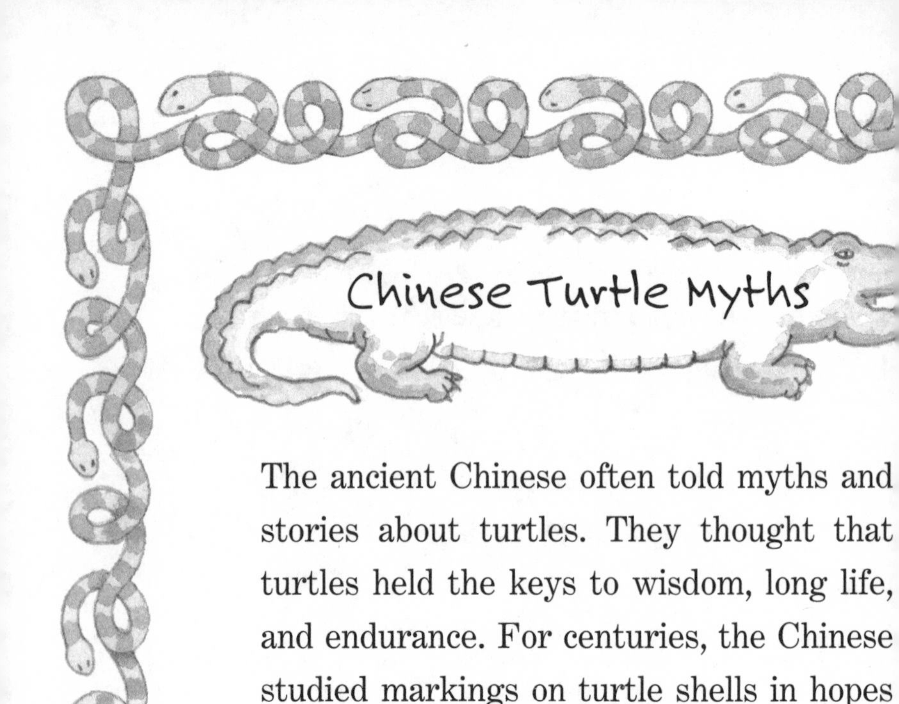

Chinese Turtle Myths

The ancient Chinese often told myths and stories about turtles. They thought that turtles held the keys to wisdom, long life, and endurance. For centuries, the Chinese studied markings on turtle shells in hopes of predicting the future.

Chinese myths say that the whole world rests on the back of a turtle. In one myth, a ruler named Fu Xi is supposed to have discovered writing by examining turtles. He believed that all the markings of heaven and earth were on their shells.

In Taiwan today, people buy turtles made out of flour. They take them home hoping that the flour turtles will give them good luck for the coming year. The Chinese also believe that patting a turtle's shell will bring good fortune.

Turn the page for a sneak peek at

Magic Tree House® #9

DOLPHINS AT DAYBREAK

Published by Random House Children's Books, a division of Penguin Random House LLC, New York.

3

Mini-Sub

"You've really done it now, Annie!" said Jack.

"Sorry, sorry. But look out the window!" Annie said. "Look!"

"Forget it! We have to figure this out!" Jack stared at the computer. He saw a row of pictures at the top of the screen.

"What did you do?" he asked.

"I just pressed the ON button," said Annie.

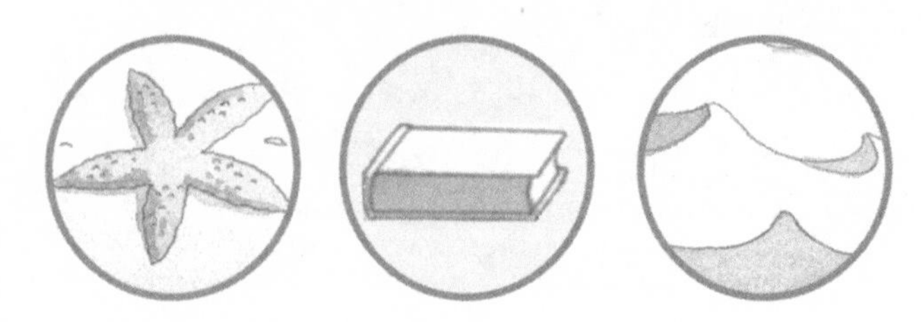

"The screen lit up. And I pressed the starfish."

"That must be the command to go under the water," said Jack.

"Yeah. Then the map came on," said Annie.

"Okay, okay. The map shows the reef," said Jack. "Look! There's the mini-sub on the map! It's moving away from the reef."

"It's like a video game," said Annie. "I bet I know what to do."

Annie pressed a key with an arrow pointing right. The mini-sub on the screen moved right. The real mini-sub turned to the right, also.

"Great!" said Jack with relief. "You press the arrows to steer the mini-sub. So now we can go back."

"Oh, no, not right away," said Annie. "It's so beautiful down here."

"We have to get back to the reef," said Jack. His eyes were still glued to the computer screen. "What if the owners find it gone?"

"Look out the window," said Annie. "Just for one teeny second."

Jack sighed. He pushed his glasses into place and looked up. "Oh, man," he said softly.

Outside the glass was a strange world of bright moving color.

It looked like another planet.

The mini-sub was moving past red, yellow, and blue coral—past little coral mountains, valleys, and caves—past fishes of every color and size.

"Can't we stay a little while? The answer to Morgan's riddle must be here," said Annie.

Jack nodded slowly. She might be right, he thought. Besides, when would they ever get to visit a place like this again?

Magic Tree House®

#1: Dinosaurs Before Dark
#2: The Knight at Dawn
#3: Mummies in the Morning
#4: Pirates Past Noon
#5: Night of the Ninjas
#6: Afternoon on the Amazon
#7: Sunset of the Sabertooth
#8: Midnight on the Moon
#9: Dolphins at Daybreak
#10: Ghost Town at Sundown
#11: Lions at Lunchtime
#12: Polar Bears Past Bedtime
#13: Vacation Under the Volcano
#14: Day of the Dragon King
#15: Viking Ships at Sunrise
#16: Hour of the Olympics
#17: Tonight on the *Titanic*
#18: Buffalo Before Breakfast
#19: Tigers at Twilight
#20: Dingoes at Dinnertime
#21: Civil War on Sunday
#22: Revolutionary War on Wednesday
#23: Twister on Tuesday
#24: Earthquake in the Early Morning
#25: Stage Fright on a Summer Night
#26: Good Morning, Gorillas
#27: Thanksgiving on Thursday
#28: High Tide in Hawaii
#29: A Big Day for Baseball
#30: Hurricane Heroes in Texas
#31: Warriors in Winter
#32: To the Future, Ben Franklin!
#33: Narwhal on a Sunny Night
#34: Late Lunch with Llamas
#35: Camp Time in California
#36: Sunlight on the Snow Leopard
#37: Rhinos at Recess
#38: Time of the Turtle King

Magic Tree House® Merlin Missions

#1: Christmas in Camelot
#2: Haunted Castle on Hallows Eve
#3: Summer of the Sea Serpent
#4: Winter of the Ice Wizard
#5: Carnival at Candlelight
#6: Season of the Sandstorms
#7: Night of the New Magicians
#8: Blizzard of the Blue Moon
#9: Dragon of the Red Dawn
#10: Monday with a Mad Genius
#11: Dark Day in the Deep Sea
#12: Eve of the Emperor Penguin
#13: Moonlight on the Magic Flute
#14: A Good Night for Ghosts
#15: Leprechaun in Late Winter
#16: A Ghost Tale for Christmas Time
#17: A Crazy Day with Cobras
#18: Dogs in the Dead of Night
#19: Abe Lincoln at Last!
#20: A Perfect Time for Pandas
#21: Stallion by Starlight
#22: Hurry Up, Houdini!
#23: High Time for Heroes
#24: Soccer on Sunday
#25: Shadow of the Shark
#26: Balto of the Blue Dawn
#27: Night of the Ninth Dragon

Magic Tree House® Super Edition

#1: World at War, 1944

Magic Tree House® Fact Trackers

Dinosaurs
Knights and Castles
Mummies and Pyramids
Pirates
Rain Forests
Space
Titanic
Twisters and Other Terrible Storms
Dolphins and Sharks
Ancient Greece and the Olympics
American Revolution
Sabertooths and the Ice Age
Pilgrims
Ancient Rome and Pompeii
Tsunamis and Other Natural Disasters
Polar Bears and the Arctic
Sea Monsters
Penguins and Antarctica
Leonardo da Vinci
Ghosts
Leprechauns and Irish Folklore
Rags and Riches: Kids in the Time of Charles Dickens
Snakes and Other Reptiles
Dog Heroes
Abraham Lincoln
Pandas and Other Endangered Species
Horse Heroes
Heroes for All Times
Soccer
Ninjas and Samurai
China: Land of the Emperor's Great Wall
Sharks and Other Predators
Vikings
Dogsledding and Extreme Sports
Dragons and Mythical Creatures
World War II
Baseball
Wild West
Texas
Warriors
Benjamin Franklin
Narwhals and Other Whales
Llamas and the Andes
Snow Leopards and Other Wild Cats

More Magic Tree House®

Games and Puzzles from the Tree House
Magic Tricks from the Tree House
My Magic Tree House Journal
Magic Tree House Survival Guide
Animal Games and Puzzles
Magic Tree House Incredible Fact Book